The Christmas Box

By JoAnne Stewart Wetzel   Illustrated by Barry Root

Alfred A. Knopf, New York

To my parents, Dorothy and Kenneth Stewart, who made Christmas
special no matter where we were; and to my brother, R. J., who
always woke me up on Christmas morning
—*J. S. W.*

For my mother
—*B. R.*

THIS IS A BORZOI BOOK PUBLISHED BY ALFRED A. KNOPF, INC.

Text copyright © 1992 by JoAnne Stewart Wetzel. Illustrations copyright © 1992 by Barrett Root.

All rights reserved under International and Pan-American Copyright Conventions.
Published in the United States by Alfred A. Knopf, Inc., New York, and
simultaneously in Canada by Random House of Canada Limited, Toronto.
Distributed by Random House, Inc., New York.

Library of Congress Cataloging-in-Publication Data
Wetzel, JoAnne Stewart.   The Christmas box / by JoAnne Stewart Wetzel ;
illustrated by Barry Root.
p.   cm.
Summary: When Father is stationed with the military in Japan, he sends his two
children an intriguing wooden box at Christmastime.
ISBN 0-679-81789-1 (trade) — ISBN 0-679-91789-6 (lib. bdg.)
[1. Christmas—Fiction. 2. Father and child—Fiction.]   I. Root, Barry, ill.   II. Title.
PZ7.W534Ch   1992   [E]—dc20   91-38911

Manufactured in the United States   10 9 8 7 6 5 4 3 2 1

Author's note

This is a true story. In 1952 my father was sent to Kyushu, Japan, with the United States Air Force. While many American families were able to live in Japan that year, there wasn't enough housing on Kyushu for everyone. This time we had to stay at home.

Many years ago, when I was young and my brother was even younger, Daddy went to Japan to be a soldier. We couldn't go with him, because there was no place for us to live. Daddy lived in a tent, and he wrote wonderful letters telling us about Japan.

He told us about the Japanese children he saw, dressed up for a holiday in their embroidered kimonos. On their feet they wore getas, which clicked as they walked.

He told us about the flowering cherry trees and Mount Fujiyama and how silly he looked when he tried to eat with chopsticks for the first time. I wished I could have seen him.

We wrote him too and told him everything that was happening at home. I told him about my birthday party and my new school, and I drew him a picture of the gypsy costume I wore for Halloween.

Ricky sent Daddy a scribble picture of himself dressed up like a cowboy. I wrote on the back to explain what it was.

When Dinah had kittens, we named one Neko, which means *cat* in Japanese. We took pictures of the kittens to send to Daddy. And lots of pictures of us.

In the middle of October we baked Christmas cookies—
gingerbread men, Russian teacakes, and snickerdoodles.
We mailed the cookies to Japan.
We sent Daddy's Christmas presents too.
Daddy wouldn't be home for Christmas.

We did the Christmas things that we always do, but without Daddy. Ricky and I sprayed white snow on the windows, while Mommy hung a wreath on the door.

Uncle Steve helped us buy our tree. We set it outside the front door, where it would wait until Christmas Eve.

We went downtown to see the Christmas windows with
Aunt Helen and our cousins. It began to snow big lazy flakes
as we were looking at the windows.

When we got home, a wooden box frosted with snow was sitting on the stoop. It was addressed to all of us and stamped "Do Not Open Until Christmas." It was from Daddy!

The box was too big to shake.

Mommy put it on the floor of the hall closet. It was exactly as tall as my red rubber boots. Sometimes I forgot Daddy wouldn't be home for Christmas, but every time I opened the closet, I remembered.

On Christmas Eve we brought the tree indoors. Soon the whole house smelled like pine.

We hung our stockings by the door, because we didn't have a fireplace.

Then we went to the Children's Service at our church.
We sang my favorite carol, "Hark! The Herald Angels Sing,"
and we sang "Silent Night." That's Daddy's favorite.

It was so hard to fall asleep that night. Everything in the
house was waiting for Christmas.

Ricky woke me as soon as the sun began
to come up, and we ran downstairs.
    The stockings bulged with mysterious lumps.
    The tree glittered and shone, presents piled beneath it in
a wonderful confusion. The wooden box was under the tree now.

We emptied our stockings before we unwrapped any presents. This year it took a long time to get to the tangerine in the toe. All of us, even Mommy, kept looking at the wooden box.

It was the first present we opened.

Inside was Japan.

There were kimonos for Ricky and me, and clicky getas to wear with them, perfumed fans painted with pictures of blossoming cherry trees and Mount Fujiyama, chopsticks to eat with, a boy doll for Ricky and a girl doll for me, and lots of presents for Mommy too.

But the best present was for all of us—a photo album filled with pictures of Daddy. Ricky and I sat on either side of Mommy as she turned the pages.

"Daddy is with us this Christmas," I said. "Isn't he?"

"Yes," said Mommy, smiling.

"I hope we're with him too," said Ricky.

We never threw away that wooden box. When Daddy came home from Japan, he gave it hinges and wheels so Ricky and I could keep our toys in it. Over the years the box was used to store all kinds of things—magazines and sewing supplies and Daddy's tools. But no matter what it held, we always called it "The Christmas Box."